# KATIE WOO

by Fran Manushkin

illustrated by Tammie Lyon

capstone

Katie Woo is published by Picture Window Books
A Capstone Imprint
1710 Roe Crest Drive
North Mankato, MN 56003
www.mycapstone.com

Text © 2013 Fran Manushkin
Illustrations © 2013 Picture Window Books

Cataloging-in-Publication Data is available on the
Library of Congress website.
ISBN: 978-1-4795-9318-7

Summary: Katie Woo knows how to make every day an adventure.
Of course, a curious, creative girl like her sometimes finds herself
in a bit of mischief, but don't worry! Katie always manages to fix
her mishaps, making her friends laugh along the way.

Photo Credits
Fran Manushkin, pg. 96; Tammie Lyon, pg. 96

Previously published in 2013 by Picture Window Books
as three separate editions:
Katie Woo Rules the School
Katie Woo and Friends
Katie Woo Celebrates

Printed and bound in China.
003971

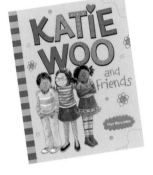

Join the adventures
of katie and
her friends.

# KATIE WOO

# WOO

## Rules the School

# Table of Contents

# Katie and the Class Pet

One day, Miss Winkle asked, "Who would like to have a class pet?"

"I would!" yelled everyone.

"I want a pony," said Katie. "We could ride him at recess!"

"A pony is too big," said Miss Winkle. "We need a pet that fits in our room."

"How about a rabbit?" asked JoJo.

"Or a mouse," said Pedro.

"I'll think about it," said Miss Winkle.

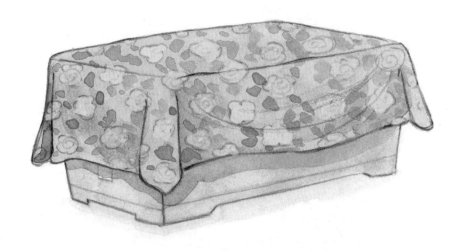

A few days later, Miss Winkle
came in with a cage.

"Our class pet is inside," she said.
"Can you guess what it is?"

"A bunch of ants?" asked Pedro.

"A skunk?" joked Barry.

"Surprise!" said Miss Winkle.
"It's a guinea pig."

"He's so cute," said JoJo.

"Let's name him Binky," said
Katie. "The name is cute and little,
like him."

"Binky! Binky! Binky!" everyone shouted.

"Binky it is!" said Miss Winkle.

Binky let everyone hold him.

He made happy, squeaky noises.

He liked being at school. He loved music time best. He always squeaked along.

Every Friday, Miss Winkle took
Binky home for the weekend. But
one Friday, she said, "I'm going away
this weekend. I need someone to take
Binky home."

"Me! Me! Me!"
yelled everyone.

Miss Winkle pulled a name from
a hat. Katie Woo won!

"Binky, I'll take good care of
you," she promised.

Katie put Binky's cage in her room.
She fed him guinea-pig pellets and
grapes and cucumbers.

Then she and Binky played games.

"Keep the doors and windows closed," said Katie's dad. "We don't want Binky to get lost."

That night, Katie fell asleep in her
bed, and Binky slept in his house.

Katie played with Binky all
weekend.

On Sunday, she said, "Binky, I'd
love to keep you, but you belong to
our class. They would miss you."

On Monday morning, Katie took Binky out of his cage one last time.

"Uh-oh," she said. "I have to go to the bathroom."

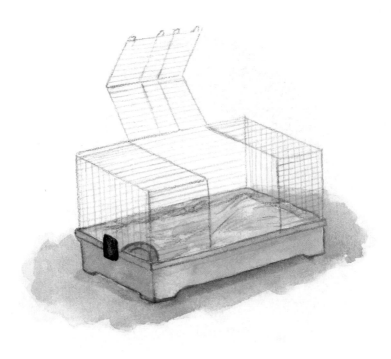

When Katie came back, Binky was gone! Katie looked under the bed and everywhere. No Binky!

The window was open a crack. "He must have escaped!" Katie cried.

Katie felt terrible. "What will I tell my class?" she said. "I promised to take good care of Binky."

Katie picked up her backpack and headed out the door.

Katie walked to her classroom
slowly. "I hope I never get there," she
said.

But she did.

Miss Winkle asked, "Katie, how was your weekend with Binky?"

"Um, I have some bad news . . ." Katie began.

Then she started to cry.

Suddenly, Katie felt something on
her neck. It was warm and soft. It was
Binky, poking out of her backpack!

"So that's where you went!" Katie
smiled. "You were getting ready to
come to school!"

"Katie," asked Miss Winkle, "what's the bad news you were going to tell us?"

"It's not bad anymore!" Katie laughed. "It's funny!"

And she told them the whole happy story.

# No More
# Teasing

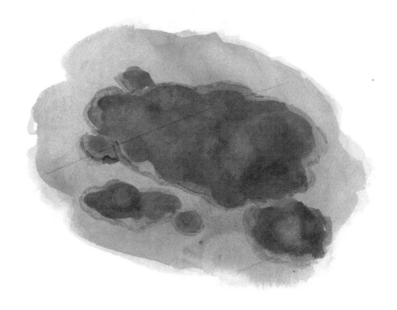

One day, on the way to school,
Katie Woo tripped. She fell into the
mud. *Splat!*

She scraped her knee, and mud
got on her new sweater and all of her
books.

Katie started to cry.

"Cry baby! Cry baby!" yelled
Roddy Rogers.

Katie's feelings were so hurt, she
cried harder.

Roddy grinned.

At school, Roddy Rogers kept
teasing Katie during recess.

"Go away!" she told him.

But Roddy didn't.

At lunch, they
had pizza, Katie's
favorite.

She took such a
big bite that she got tomato
sauce on her nose and cheek.

"Look at Katie," Roddy shouted. "Katie's got a goopy face!"

Roddy said, "Goopy face! Goopy face!"

"Stop it!" cried Katie. But Roddy didn't stop. He was having too much fun.

Roddy made faces
at Katie all day long.
When Katie stuck
her tongue out at
him, he made
more faces. Ugly ones.

"How can I make Roddy stop teasing me?" Katie asked her friend JoJo.

But JoJo didn't know.

The next day, Roddy teased Katie
when she was running at recess. And
he teased her when she was trying to
read her book.

Katie was so unhappy. She didn't
want to go to school anymore.

The next day, Miss Winkle told the class, "Everyone, our butterflies are ready to hatch. Please hurry over and watch them!"

Katie pushed up her glasses.

"Hey, I see four eyes!" Roddy said in a quiet voice. He knew if Miss Winkle heard him, he would get in trouble.

Katie was about to say something
back. But suddenly, her butterfly
began hatching.

It was so amazing. She couldn't
take her eyes off it!

Roddy said, "Four eyes!" a little louder.

But Katie kept watching her butterfly.

Roddy was so mad. He slammed his desk and hurt his finger.

Later, the class worked on their "Good Neighbors" paintings with a partner.

Roddy snuck over to Katie and said, "Ew! Your painting is ugly!"

But Katie loved painting so much
that she kept doing it.

"Hey!" Roddy said. "Didn't you
hear me?"

Katie still didn't answer.

Roddy got so mad that he smeared black paint all over his part of his picture.

"Hey!" his partner yelled. "You ruined our painting!"

On the way home, Roddy glared at
Katie, but she didn't even look at him.

Katie began smiling and smiling.

When JoJo sat down, Katie told

her, "I'm so happy! I know how to

make Roddy stop teasing me."

"What do you do?" asked JoJo.

"Nothing!" Katie said. "When I don't cry or yell, Roddy isn't having fun, so he stops teasing me."

"Katie Woo, you are one smart girl," said JoJo.

"Thanks!" said Katie. And she smiled all the way home.

# The Big Lie

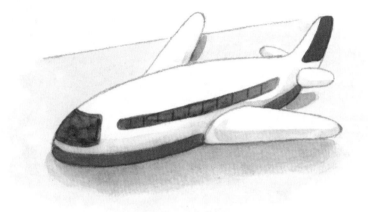

One day after recess, Miss Winkle told the class, "Jake has lost his toy airplane. Has anybody found it?"

Katie Woo shook her head no. So did her friends Pedro and JoJo and everyone else.

"My father gave me the airplane yesterday," said Jake.

"It was a birthday present,"
he said.

"Maybe your plane flew away,"
said someone else.

"That is not funny," said Miss
Winkle.

JoJo told Jake, "I saw you playing with your plane at recess. It's so neat! I hope you find it."

Miss Winkle asked again, "Does anyone know where Jake's airplane is?"

"I don't," Katie told Jake. But she was lying.

Earlier that day during recess, Katie saw Jake running around with his airplane.

"I want to do that!" Katie told herself. "I wish that plane belonged to me."

When recess was almost over, three fire trucks sped by.

While everyone was
watching them and
waving to the firefighters,
Katie grabbed Jake's plane.
She put it into her pocket.

Now Jake's plane was inside
Katie's desk.

"I can't wait to play with it when
I go home," Katie thought.

During art class, Katie said,
"Maybe a kangaroo hopped over and
put the airplane in her pouch."

"I don't think so," said Miss
Winkle. "There are no kangaroos
around here."

During spelling, Katie said,
"Maybe the garbage man came and
took Jake's plane."

"No way!" JoJo said. She shook her
head. "I didn't see any garbage trucks."

Jake kept staring at the empty
box that his airplane came in. The
birthday ribbon was still on the box.

Jake looked like he was going
to cry.

Katie didn't feel happy either.

When nobody was looking, she took something out of her desk and put it into her pocket.

Katie walked to the window and began using the pencil sharpener.

All of a sudden, Katie yelled, "I see Jake's plane. It's by the window! It must have flown in during recess."

Katie handed Jake the plane.

She whispered, "That was a lie, Jake.

I took your plane, and I am very sorry!"

At first, Jake was angry at Katie. Then he said, "I am glad you gave it back. I feel a lot better now."

"I do too!" Katie said.

And that was the truth.

# Star of
the Show

Katie's class was putting on a play.

"We're doing *The Princess and the Frog*," said Miss Winkle.

"Hooray!" said Katie. "I want to be the princess!"

"Me too!" yelled JoJo.

"I want to be the
frog," said Pedro. "I'm
a great hopper!"

"The parts are
on these cards," said
Miss Winkle. "Pick
one to see which part you get."

Katie picked
her card first.

"Oh, no!" she
groaned. "I'm not the
princess. I'm a worm!"

"I'm the princess!" yelled JoJo.

"And I'm the frog!" said Pedro.

"Good for you," said Katie. But she felt sad. "A worm cannot be a star," she sighed.

Katie told her dad, "It's no fun to
be a worm. All I do is wiggle."

Her dad said, "You are crafty,
Katie. You'll be a great worm."

Katie asked her mom, "What does crafty mean?"

"It means clever," said her mom. "I know you will be the best worm you can be!"

Katie tried to be a great worm.

She worked hard on her wiggling.

She wiggled forward, and she wiggled

backward.

Pedro and JoJo worked hard on their parts, too.

JoJo told Pedro, "Don't forget to kiss me so you can turn into a prince."

Pedro nodded. "Sure, sure."

The big day came, and the curtain
went up.

"This is so exciting!" said Katie.

"Oh, Frog," called the princess.
"I threw my golden ball into the well.
Will you get it for me?"

"Sure!" croaked the frog. He began
hopping to the well.

"I can't see anything in my
costume," said Katie.

She wiggled close to Pedro and
almost tripped him!

"Oops," she thought. "That was
not crafty."

"Thank you for bringing me
my golden ball," said the princess.

"Uh-oh," Katie whispered.
"The tree is swaying! It's going to
fall down!"

Katie wiggled over and leaned on the tree.

"Stop that!" hissed the tree. "I'm swaying in the wind! I'm not falling down!"

It was time for
the frog to kiss the
princess, but the
frog didn't move.
He looked scared.

"Kiss her!"
whispered Miss Winkle.

The frog still did not move. But
Katie did!

She wiggled over and whispered,
"If you don't kiss the princess, this
worm will kiss YOU!"

"EW!" said Pedro.

He kissed the princess.

"You are now a prince!" she said.

The audience clapped and cheered,

"Hurray!"

As the princess took a bow, her crown fell off — and landed on the worm's head!

Katie smiled and
wiggled. Everyone clapped
harder! So Katie took a big
bow.

After the show, Pedro said, "Katie, you were so clever! You scared me into kissing JoJo."

"Well," said Katie, "I wanted you to be the best frog you could be."

"And you were the craftiest worm," said Katie's dad.

"I guess a worm CAN be a star!" said Katie.

And everybody agreed.

# KATIE WOO

# and Friends

# Table of Contents

# Boss of
# the World

Katie Woo and her friends took a trip to the beach.

"Let's do everything together!" said Katie. "We'll have so much fun!"

"Let's build the
biggest sand castle in
the world!" shouted
Pedro.

"You two carry the water to me.
I will build the castle," said Katie.

"That's not fun!" JoJo said.

"I think it is," replied Katie.

When the castle was finished, it
wasn't very big, and it kept falling
down.

"What a rotten castle!" Katie
moaned.

At lunchtime, Katie shouted, "I'm so hungry, I could eat an elephant!"

"Me too!" said JoJo and Pedro.

They passed French fries around, but Katie ate most of them.

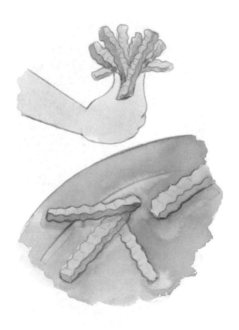

JoJo and Pedro had only three fries each.

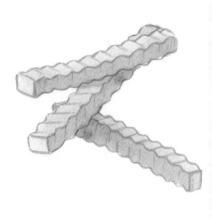

"I'm still hungry," said Pedro.

Katie grinned. "I'm not!" she said.

After lunch, Katie said, "Let's lie on the blanket. We can watch the clouds and kites flying by."

"Katie, move over!" Pedro said.
"You are taking up all of the blanket!"

"It's my blanket," Katie said. She
did not move one inch. Pedro and JoJo
had to lie on the itchy sand.

"Let's go over to the playground," Pedro said. "There are big swings there."

The three friends raced each other. Katie got there first and grabbed the only empty swing.

JoJo and Pedro watched her swinging for a while. Then they walked away.

"What's wrong with them?" Katie wondered.

She ran after her
friends, saying, "Let's
look for seashells!"

The three friends
took off their shoes. They walked
barefoot along the shore. The waves
tickled their toes.

"I see a giant shell!" Pedro shouted.

He began running. But he tripped over some driftwood and fell down.

Katie grabbed the seashell.

"Hey, that's not fair!" said JoJo.
"Pedro saw the giant shell first."

"Finders keepers," Katie insisted.

JoJo and Pedro made faces and
walked away.

Katie grabbed her beach ball and began tossing it around, but it wasn't any fun.

Just then, JoJo and Pedro and JoJo's dad began swimming and splashing around in the waves.

Katie ran over, shouting, "I want to swim too!"

"No!" yelled JoJo. "You can't! The sea belongs to us!"

"That's silly," Katie said. She laughed. "The sea can't belong to you."

"And all the French fries don't belong to you," said Pedro.

"And all the seashells," added JoJo.

"And the blankets and swings," said Pedro.

"Uh-oh!" said Katie Woo. "I think I have been a meanie."

"For sure!" said Pedro and JoJo.

"I'm sorry!" said Katie. "I won't be a meanie anymore. Is it okay if I share the sea with you?"

"Yes!" said her friends.

And there were plenty of waves for everyone!

# The Tricky Tooth

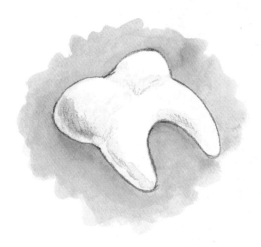

"Guess what?" Katie told JoJo. "I have a loose tooth!"

"So do I," said JoJo. "If we wiggle them, they might come out."

Katie wiggled her tooth back
tand forth.

So did JoJo.

"No luck," said JoJo.

"No luck," sighed Katie.

"Let's eat a lot of
popcorn," said Katie.
"That will make our
teeth come out."

The two of them
chewed and chewed. JoJo's tooth
fell out!

But Katie's stayed put.

At bedtime, Katie brushed her tooth
a lot, but it didn't fall out.

"No tooth for the Tooth Fairy," Katie
sighed.

The next day, Miss Winkle asked
Katie's class, "Who has lost a tooth?"
Everyone raised their hands.
Everyone but Katie.

After school, Katie played soccer. She told Pedro, "I'll hit the ball with my head. That will make my tooth come out!"

"I love the space between my teeth," Pedro said. "It helps me whistle really loud!"

Katie sighed. "I want a space, too."

When the ball came to Katie, she
bumped it hard. She scored a goal!
But her tooth did not budge.

The next day, Katie
lost a sock, a button,
and her pencil.

But she did not
lose her tooth.

Katie's mom said, "Don't worry.
Your tooth will come out when it's
ready."

"I'm ready now!" said Katie.

Katie went to dance class. She
jumped and spun around. She got
very dizzy, but her tooth didn't move.

At school, Miss Winkle made a
tooth chart. "Put a check on it for
each tooth you have lost," she said.
Katie had no checks.

At home, Katie told her dad, "I'd like to be a blue whale. They don't have any teeth to worry about."

"That's not a good idea," teased her dad. "Our bathtub isn't big enough."

Katie's mom told Katie, "It's a mystery how teeth come out."

"It sure is," Katie groaned. "This tooth is tricky!"

The phone rang. It was Pedro. He asked Katie, "When can you come to see my new puppy?"

"Right now!" said Katie. "That will cheer me up!"

Pedro's puppy was adorable! "His name is Toto," said Pedro.

"Like in *The Wizard of Oz*," said Katie. "Cool!"

"Can I hold Toto?" Katie asked.

"Sure!" Pedro nodded. "Just be gentle."

Toto was so warm and soft, Katie nuzzled him with her cheek.

"Arf!" The puppy barked and
nuzzled Katie back.

"Hey," said Katie, "I feel
something on my tongue."

"It's my tooth!" Katie yelled.
"Way to go, Toto!"

"Way to go, Katie!" said Pedro.
"Now you have a space, too."

Katie couldn't stop smiling!

That night, Katie put the tooth under her pillow.

"Don't fall out or anything," she said. "I want the Tooth Fairy to find you."

And the Tooth Fairy did.

# Goodbye to Goldie

Katie Woo's dog, Goldie, was very old.

One day, Goldie
became very sick. A
week later, she died.
Katie's mom held
Katie while she cried.

"I will miss Goldie so much," Katie cried. "She was my best friend."

Katie's friend JoJo hugged her. "I
will miss Goldie too," said JoJo. "She
was the nicest dog in the world."

"She was!" agreed Pedro.

"Goldie loved running on the beach," said Pedro.

"We didn't have to go into the sea to get wet," said JoJo. "Goldie would just shake her fur and make us all wet!"

"Goldie was great in the snow, too!" said Pedro. "We used to toss snowballs, and she would try to catch them in her mouth."

"Tell me some more happy stories about Goldie," said Katie.

JoJo grinned. "That's easy! There are so many."

"At Thanksgiving, Goldie ate my drumstick," JoJo said. "I turned around, and it was gone!"

"Goldie was smart," said Katie. "And fast!"

"Goldie was so much fun on
Halloween," said Katie. "Remember
the time she wore a skunk costume?
She ran around and scared all the
other dogs!"

"Goldie loved
tickling my face with
her tail," said JoJo.

"She dusted the
table with it too,"
joked Katie's mom.

"And my computer!" added
Katie's dad.

"Her tail hardly ever
stopped wagging," said
Katie.

"Goldie and I were both scared of thunder," said Katie. "But when we hugged, we both felt better."

"Goldie was a good cuddler," agreed Katie's mom.

Katie's dad showed her a photo.
It was taken when she and Goldie
were little. They were eating hot dogs
together.

"This photo is great," Katie said.
"I love looking at it."

JoJo had an idea. "We should make Katie a Goldie scrapbook. She can look at it whenever she feels sad."

Katie's mom found two photos of Goldie and Katie. In one, they were playing catch with a ball.

In the other, they were both very small. They were taking a nap on the grass.

Katie drew a picture of Goldie catching popcorn in her mouth.

"She was good at that!" Katie said, smiling. "She never missed!"

"Goldie could jump
rope too," said JoJo.
"And kick a soccer
ball!"

"And almost catch
squirrels!" added Pedro.

Chasing Squirrels

"Goldie lived a long and happy
life," said Katie's mom.

"She sure did," said Katie.

That night at
bedtime, Katie held
Goldie's picture and
kissed it good night.

"Goldie, I will always remember you," Katie promised.

And she always did.

# Katie Goes Camping

Katie was going camping.

"I know all about camping," she told Pedro and JoJo. "It's so much fun!"

Soon they reached the woods.

"First, we put up our tent," said Katie.

"Watch out!" said JoJo. "It's falling down."

"I can fix it," said Pedro.

"Way to go!" said JoJo.

"Now, let's explore!" Katie said.

"I will show you the pond."

"The pond is the other way." JoJo pointed.

"No, it's not!" insisted Katie.

Katie ran down the path, but soon she was alone. No Pedro! No JoJo! No pond!

"I am not scared," Katie said.

She climbed a rock and looked around. She saw JoJo and Pedro coming.

"Boo!" Katie yelled.

JoJo jumped. "Katie, you scared me!"

"I'm very wild!" Katie bragged.

"It's raining," Pedro said.

Soon the rain stopped, and the sun came out.

"Look!" Katie pointed. "There's a rainbow! Let's make wishes on it."

Later, Katie's dad made a campfire, and they cooked hot dogs and marshmallows.

"Camping is tasty!" said JoJo.

Soon it was dark.
Stars filled the sky,
and fireflies filled the
grass.

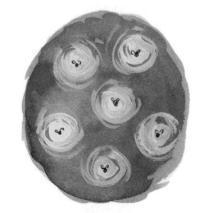

"I'd like to glow at
night," joked Katie.

"Me too!" said Pedro. "Then I'd
never get lost."

"I know a ghost story," said Katie's dad. "Once upon a time, there was a bloody finger."

"Stop!" yelled JoJo. "That's scary."

When they were in their tent,
Pedro asked, "Are there bears around
here?"

"I hope not!" said JoJo.

"I hope we see one," said Katie.

Soon Pedro and JoJo fell asleep, but Katie did not.

She was thirsty, so she tiptoed out of the tent.

Then Pedro woke up.

He was thirsty too, so he tiptoed
out of the tent.

Then JoJo woke up.

"Where is everyone?" she said.

"I don't want to be alone."

She tiptoed out of the tent.

It was very dark.

"Oh no!" said Katie. "I see a bear
— with antlers."

Katie began running.

Pedro saw something dark. "It's a ghost!" he yelled.

Pedro began running!

JoJo turned on her flashlight.

"I don't see a ghost!" She

laughed. "I see Katie and Pedro

chasing each other!"

"I wasn't scared," Katie insisted.

"And I wasn't!" said Pedro.

"Oh sure." JoJo laughed.

Back in the tent, JoJo asked Pedro and Katie, "What did you wish on the rainbow?"

"I wished I could see a ghost," said Pedro.

"You did," said Katie. "Almost!"

"I wished to go camping again," said JoJo.

"That's an easy wish to get!" Katie smiled.

"I wished I was a better camper," Katie said.

"You are a great camper!" Pedro laughed. "You are so much fun!"

"My dog likes camping with you too," said JoJo.

"Arf!" JoJo's dog agreed.

Then all the campers fell asleep.

# KATIE WOO

# Celebrates

# Table of Contents

# No Valentines for Katie

It was a cold gray day, but Katie was happy. It was Valentine's Day!

At school, Miss Winkle said, "Let's start the day with a valentine math puzzle."

"Take out your crayons, and draw a big heart. Then try to guess how many candy hearts will fit inside of it."

Katie drew a big red heart. Then she looked at the tiny candy hearts.

One said, "Puppy Love." Another said, "Melt My Heart."

"I think this heart will hold twelve candies," Katie decided. But when she filled up the heart, it held twenty.

"Boy, did I guess wrong!" Katie said.

"I love these tiny hearts," she said, smiling.

She couldn't stop reading them. She read "Cloud Nine" and "Soul Mate."

Miss Winkle said, "Now print your name on a piece of paper, and put it in the valentine box."

Then the class went out for recess.

When they came back, Miss

Winkle said, "Now the real fun starts!"

"Take out a piece of paper from the valentine box. You will make a valentine for the person that you pick," said Miss Winkle.

Katie picked Barry, the new boy.
As Katie began painting, Miss
Winkle said, "Each valentine should
say something nice about the person."

Katie whispered to JoJo, "I wonder
who made me a valentine? I can't wait
to see what it says about me!"

Ella read her card first. "This valentine is for Pedro. I like you because you are a great goalie! When we play soccer, you know how to use your head!"

"Thanks!" Pedro said.

Charlotte read her valentine.
"JoJo, I like you because you jump
rope so fast! And when I forget to
bring my lunch, you share yours
with me."

"Thank you!" said JoJo, beaming.

One by one, the students read their valentines. But nobody read one for Katie.

Katie's eyes filled with tears. "Someone got my name," she said, "but I guess they couldn't think of anything nice to say. That's why I didn't get a card."

"Katie," said Miss Winkle, "are you
sure you put your name into the box?"

"Oh, no!" Katie groaned. "I forgot!
I was so busy reading my candy
hearts."

"Well," said Miss Winkle, "since
Katie did not get a card, will someone
come up to the board and write
something nice about her?"

"I will!" said Barry, the new boy.

He wrote, "I think Katie is very funny. And her glasses are just like mine!"

Katie smiled. "Thank you!" she said.

Now Barry looked sad. "I didn't get a card," he said.

Katie jumped up. "I got your name!" she said.

"Barry, I don't know you very well,
but I think you are funny! Plus you
have the same glasses as me!"

Barry couldn't stop smiling. "Katie,
we said the same things!"

After school, Katie said, "Barry, can you walk home with us?"

"Sure," he agreed. "Do you promise to be funny?"

"I always am!" said Katie.

And they laughed together all the way home.

# Red, White, and Blue, and Katie Woo!

"The Fourth of July is my favorite holiday!" said Katie Woo.

JoJo laughed. "Katie, you say that about every holiday!"

"I guess I do," Katie said with a smile. "But the Fourth of July is the best! We're having a parade and a party in my backyard."

"And don't forget the fireworks," said Pedro.

Katie and Pedro and JoJo put red, white, and blue decorations on their bikes.

Everyone cheered when they rode
by in the parade.

"Way to go!" yelled Katie's mom
and dad.

After the parade, they went back to
Katie's house. Pedro said, "Katie, your
yard is so big, we can play soccer in it."

Katie kicked the ball hard.

"I can get it!" yelled Pedro. He backed up to hit the ball with his head.

Oops! Pedro tripped over the table
and fell down. He spilled cherry soda
all over his head!

"No points for you!" yelled Katie
Woo.

"The hot dogs are ready," called
her dad. "Where are the buns?"

"Uh-oh!" Katie groaned. "JoJo's dog ate them!"

The hot dogs looked lonely without buns.

Katie's mom put out big bowls
of strawberries and blueberries and
whipped cream.

"We'll eat this later," she said. "It
will be our dessert."

"I'd like to eat it now," said JoJo.

"Come on," Katie said. "Let's play ringtoss."

The three friends tossed red, white, and blue hoops at stakes in the ground.

"I keep missing!" said JoJo. She cheered herself up by eating a few blueberries. Whenever she missed, JoJo ate some more.

Pedro won the ringtoss game.

"Uh-oh," JoJo groaned. "I think
I ate too many blueberries. I have a
stomachache."

Then it began to rain!

"Oh, no!" Katie groaned. "No fireworks!"

They began bringing all the food inside.

Katie carried the
whipped cream.

"I'd like a little
taste," Katie decided.
She pressed the button
hard — too hard!

Whipped cream
sprayed everywhere! JoJo's dog
licked it up.

"Our Fourth of July party is truly
red, white, and blue," said Katie.
"Pedro turned red when he spilled
cherry soda on his head. I am white
because I'm covered with whipped
cream."

"And I felt blue," said JoJo, "from
eating too many blueberries."

"Look," said Pedro, "the rain stopped."

"Yay!" cheered Katie. "There will be fireworks!"

"First, let's have dessert," said
Katie's mom.

"I'll skip the blueberries," decided
JoJo.

The three friends sat together in the backyard.

"What color will the fireworks be?" asked Pedro.

"Red, white, and blue!" said Katie.

And she was right.

# Boo,
# Katie Woo!

Halloween was coming.

Katie asked Pedro and JoJo,

"What are you going to be?"

"I'm going to be a cowgirl," said JoJo.

"I'm going to be a magician," said Pedro. "What are you going to be, Katie?"

"A monster!" shouted Katie. "I'll scare everyone silly!"

Finally, it was Halloween!

Katie, Pedro, and JoJo went

trick-or-treating together.

Katie rang the first bell. A girl answered.

"Boo!" shouted Katie Woo.

The girl laughed. "You don't scare me!" she said.

"I can do a trick!" said JoJo.

She twirled her cowgirl rope and jumped in and out of it.

"Cool!" said the girl. She gave JoJo lots of candy.

Katie, Pedro, and JoJo went to the
next house. A boy answered this time.

"Boo!" shouted Katie Woo.

"You don't scare me!" said the boy.

"I can do a magic trick," said
Pedro.

He made a spoon
bend by just looking
at it!

"Cool trick!" The boy smiled. He
gave Pedro a lot of candy.

As they walked to the next house, their friend Jake came running by.

"Have you seen a little brown kitten?" he asked. "She ran away, and I can't find her."

"We haven't," said Katie. "I'm sorry."

Just then, the three friends heard a spooky shriek!

"Yikes!" yelled JoJo.

"Don't be scared," said Katie. "It's only a squeaky gate swinging in the wind."

As they walked along, Katie said,
"I'm not having any fun. I haven't
scared anyone."

At the next house, Katie yelled "BOO!" as loud as she could.

"Hi, Katie!" said Barry, a boy in her class. "I knew it was you!"

Katie was so mad, she stomped her feet.

"Look!" said Pedro. "The moon is out. It looks nice and spooky."

"It's too spooky!" said JoJo with a shiver.

"Yikes!" yelled Katie. "Something's wiggling on the ground."

"It's a snake!" she screamed.

Katie climbed up a tree to get away.

"That's not a snake," said JoJo. "It's the shadow of my jump rope."

"Meow!" came a sound close to Katie in the tree.

"It's Jake's lost kitten," Katie said. "It's a good thing I climbed this tree!"

"Don't be scared," Katie told the kitten. "I'm going to take you home."

Jake hugged his kitten over and over. "How did you find her?" he asked.

Katie smiled. "Let's just say it was a trick that turned into a treat."

It was a very happy Halloween!

# Katie Saves Thanksgiving

It was Thanksgiving Day. Snow was falling. Lots and lots of snow.

"I can't wait for JoJo and Pedro to come over," said Katie. "This will be our first Thanksgiving together."

"I know a lot about the Pilgrims," Katie told her dad.

"Tell me about them," he said.

"It took a long time for the
Pilgrims to cross the sea," said Katie.
"And their ship, the *Mayflower*, went
through scary storms."

"JoJo and her family are driving through a snowstorm," said Katie. "I hope they don't get lost."

"Oh no!" said Katie's mom. "The stove isn't working!"

Katie's dad tried to fix it, but he couldn't.

"The Pilgrims had to eat cold food on the *Mayflower*," said Katie. "Their ship was made of wood. It could burn if they lit a fire."

"Maybe Pedro's family can bring some hot food," said Katie's mom.

She called them, but nobody was home.

"They must be on their way here," said Katie.

"I'll call JoJo," Katie said.

JoJo answered right away.

"Guess what?" said JoJo. "Our car is stuck in the snow! We're waiting for a tow truck."

"This is some Thanksgiving!" said Katie's dad when he heard the news.

"Without the stove, we cannot have sweet potatoes," said Katie's mom.

"Or pumpkin pie," her dad groaned.

"The snow is piling up," said

Katie's dad. "I'd better go shovel it."

"I'll help you," said Katie.

Katie and her dad began to shovel.

"Mrs. West lives alone," said Katie.

"I'll shovel her sidewalk for her."

After a while, Mrs. West called
out, "Katie, thank you for your help.
Come inside. I made some hot cocoa."

Mrs. West's kitchen was filled with wonderful smells. "I made Thanksgiving dinner for my family," she said.

Just then her
phone rang. As Mrs.
West listened, her
face grew sadder and
sadder.

She told Katie, "My family was going to take an airplane here. But it's a bad day for flying. I guess I will be eating all alone."

Katie looked out the window. She
saw JoJo and Pedro.

Katie said, "Mrs. West, why don't
you come over and eat with us?"

"What a wonderful idea!" said Mrs. West.

"Um," said Katie, "could you bring your turkey and sweet potatoes? Our stove isn't working."

"I would love to!" said Mrs. West.

Katie and JoJo and Pedro helped Mrs. West carry the food to Katie's house.

"This is just like the first Thanksgiving," said Katie. "The Pilgrims and the Indians shared their food, too."

"But they didn't have my pumpkin pie," said Mrs. West.

"But WE do!" said Katie.

Everyone was very thankful!

# Having Fun with Katie Woo!

## A Guinea Pig of Your Own

With this fun project you can make your own guinea pig out of an old sock and some dryer lint! Sounds crazy, right? But your pet will be *so* cute. I promise!

### What you need:

- an old, short sock
- stuffing, like cotton balls or fiberfill
- a needle
- thread
- craft glue

- dryer lint (Ask a grown-up where to find this soft, fuzzy stuff. It comes out of your clothes dryer!)
- googly eyes

- dark marker

## What you do:

1. Fill your sock with stuffing. This will be your guinea pig's body, so make it as fat as you would like.

2. Tuck the top of the sock in, and then ask a grown-up to sew the hole shut with a needle and thread.

3. Working in small sections, apply some craft glue to the sock. Then cover the glue with dryer lint. Repeat until the whole sock is covered. Let dry.

4. To finish your project, glue googly eyes on your pet. With the marker, draw a nose on your pet.

You can even make your guinea pig a little bed lined with shredded paper, grass, or hay. Be sure to give your pet lots of love, but don't worry about feeding it!

# Finger Puppet Fun!

Have you ever put on a puppet show? It is lots of fun and all of your friends will love it! Don't have any puppets? No problem! You can make your own. Choose from unique creatures or simple animals. It's up to you! Here's how . . .

## What you need:

- Pipe cleaners in several colors
- Small pom-poms in several colors
- Small googly eyes
- Craft glue
- Wire cutters or scissors

## What you do:

1. Firmly wrap a pipe cleaner around your finger to form the body. As you near your finger tip, make the coils smaller until the finger tip is covered. Carefully slip your finger out.

2. Glue a pom-pom onto the top of the body. You may need to hold it there while it dries.

3. Now glue two googly eyes onto the pom-pom.

4. Finally, add arms, ears, beaks, or other details using pieces of pipe cleaners. Cut the pipe cleaner with a wire cutter or scissors. Fold the pieces into the shape you want. Then glue or twist them onto your puppet. Try making a cat with short pointy ears, a rabbit with long ears, or a bird with wings and a beak.

Make two or three puppets, then act out a story with them. Your friends and family will love to watch your puppet show!

# Toothy Treats

The best treats are ones that make you smile . . .
or in this case, ones that actually *are* smiles. Apples,
peanut butter, and marshmallows come together to
make a yummy, "toothy" treat. Before your start,
wash your hands and ask a grown-up for help.

## Ingredients:

- an apple
- peanut butter
- about 40 mini marshmallows

## Other things you need:

- cutting board
- apple slicer
- paring knife
- butter knife

*Makes eight mouths

## What you do:

1. Setting the apple down on the cutting board, use the apple slicer to cut the apple into eight equal slices.

2. Take each slice of apple, and cut it in half. You now have 16 pieces.

3. Spread one side of an apple slice with peanut butter. Place four to five marshmallows on top of the peanut butter.

4. Spread peanut butter on a second slice of apple. Place the peanut-butter side down on top of the marshmallows. Now you have a toothy grin!

Repeat until you have used all your apple slices. This is a tasty treat that is healthy, too!

## About the Author

Fran Manushkin is the author of many popular picture books, including *Baby, Come Out!; Latkes and Applesauce: A Hanukkah Story; The Tushy Book; The Belly Book; and Big Girl Panties*. There is a real Katie Woo — she's Fran's great-niece — but she never gets in half the trouble of the Katie Woo in the books. Fran writes on her beloved Mac computer in New York City, without the help of her two naughty cats, Chaim and Goldy.

## About the Illustrator

Tammie Lyon began her love for drawing at a young age while sitting at the kitchen table with her dad. She continued her love of art and eventually attended the Columbus College of Art and Design, where she earned a bachelors degree in fine art. After a brief career as a professional ballet dancer, she decided to devote herself full time to illustration. Today she lives with her husband, Lee, in Cincinnati, Ohio. Her dogs, Gus and Dudley, keep her company as she works in her studio.